Teddy on Time

Written by Michael J. Pellowski
Illustrated by Len Epstein

Troll Associates

Library of Congress Cataloging in Publication Data

Pellowski, Michael.
   Teddy on time.

   Summary: Even though his alarm clock didn't awaken
him on time, Teddy Bear determines not to be late for
his special friend's party.
   [1. Teddy bears—Fiction. 2. Time—Fiction.
3. Friendship—Fiction] I. Epstein, Len, ill.
II. Title.
PZ7.P3656Te   1986   [E]   85-14127
ISBN 0-8167-0582-8 (lib. bdg.)
ISBN 0-8167-0583-6 (pbk.)

Teddy on Time

Do you like to be on time?
Teddy Bear liked to be on time.

But Teddy was not always on time. Sometimes he was late.

Why was Teddy late? Because
he did not get up on time. Why
did he not get up? Because his
alarm clock did not always
work. It was not a very good
clock.

Today Teddy wanted to be on
time. It was a special day.
Today was the day Bob Badger
was having a party. Bob told
Teddy to be on time for the
party. He told Teddy not
to be late.

But Teddy's clock didn't work.
The alarm did not ring. Teddy
did not get up on time. He slept
and slept.

9

Finally, Teddy's eyes opened.
"Oh no," he cried. "My clock
did not work. It is late. I will be
late for Bob's party."

He jumped out of bed.
"I must hurry," Teddy cried.
"To get to the party on time I
must hurry."

Teddy Bear hurried and
hurried.
"I hope I am not late for the
bus," Teddy said. "To get to the
party I must go on the bus."

"Go! Go! Go!" Teddy said. "If I am late, the bus will go. And if it goes, I will not get to the party. Hurry! Hurry! Hurry!"

Away he ran to the bus stop.
But Teddy did not hurry fast
enough.

14

The bus was at the bus stop. It was about to leave. Teddy saw the bus.

"Stop!" he yelled. "Do not go!
Do not go without me."

But the bus did go. It did not
stop for Teddy. Away it went.

"Oh no!" Teddy cried.
He ran by the bus stop.
"Stop!" he yelled.

Did the bus stop? No! The bus
kept going. It went faster and
faster. Away it went without
Teddy.

The bus was gone! There were
no more buses. Teddy Bear was
going to be late.

"Why run?" said Teddy. "The
bus is gone. I cannot get to the
party."
Teddy stopped running.

Teddy thought about Bob Badger.
"Bob is a special friend," he
said. "He told me to be on time.
Bob will not be happy."
Teddy thought and thought.

"It is a special day," said Teddy.
"I want to go to the party.
I want to be on time."

Teddy thought some more.
"I *will* go!" Teddy yelled. "I
will not be late! I will get to
Bob's party some way."

Off went Teddy Bear in a hurry.
"I will run," Teddy said. "I will
run to the party."
And run he did!

Teddy Bear ran fast. He ran
and ran.

But bears are not good runners.
Soon Teddy had to stop.
"I have run enough," Teddy
said. "I must find a new way to
be on time."

Hop! Hop! Hop! Betty Bunny
went by. She was hopping. A
bunny likes to hop. Betty Bunny
was hopping on a pogo stick. A
pogo stick is good for hopping
fast.

Teddy saw Betty. Betty saw
Teddy. The bunny stopped.

"I am late for a special party,"
said Teddy. "I cannot run to the
party. Can I have your pogo
stick? On it I can hop to the
party fast."
Betty Bunny liked Teddy Bear.
"You are a good friend," she
said. "You can have my pogo
stick. Happy hopping!"

31

Teddy Bear hopped on the pogo
stick. Hop! Hop! Hop!

Teddy hopped fast. He did not
want to be late.

But the pogo stick was big
trouble. A bunny is a good
hopper. A bear is not a good
hopper. Teddy Bear was not
good at hopping on a pogo stick.
He could not stop.

"Enough!" yelled Teddy Bear.
"Stop!"
Hop! Hop!
"Stop! Stop!" Teddy cried.
But Teddy could not stop
hopping. The pogo stick would
not stop.

Then the pogo stick stuck!
Suddenly, the hopping stopped.
Teddy Bear stopped, too!

The pogo stick fell. Teddy Bear
fell, too! Oh, what a fall! Oh,
what an unhappy Teddy Bear!

Teddy got up.
"Am I seeing things?" he cried.
What did Teddy see?
"It's the bus!" said Teddy.

The bus had stopped. It was in
trouble. The bus was stuck. It
was getting unstuck.
"Stop!" Teddy yelled. "Do not
go. I want to get on the bus."

This time the bus did not go
without Teddy. Teddy got on
the bus.
"Hurry," said Teddy. "It is late.
I have to get to a special party."

Getting stuck had made the bus late. Now that it was unstuck, the bus hurried. It hurried and hurried.

Teddy got to Bob Badger's
party. He got there fast. But
was he on time?

All of Teddy's friends were
already at the party.
"Oh no!" yelled Teddy. "Am I late?"

Teddy Bear saw Bob Badger.
Teddy went up to his friend.
"I did not want to be late," he
said. "But my clock did not
work."

"What?" said Bob Badger.
"Then the bus did not stop!"
said Teddy. "I could not run
fast enough. And I could not
hop on bunny's pogo stick."

Teddy stopped. Then he
went on.
"The pogo stick fell. But,
finally, I got on the unstuck bus.
Bob, I do not like to be late. But
sometimes I am. Today I am
late!"

"Oh no," said Bob Badger. "You
cannot be late for this party. It
is a party for a special friend. It
is a party for you! And here is a
present!"

"A new alarm clock!" cried
Teddy. "Now I will always be
on time!"
"Hooray!" shouted Teddy's
friends.
And the party began.